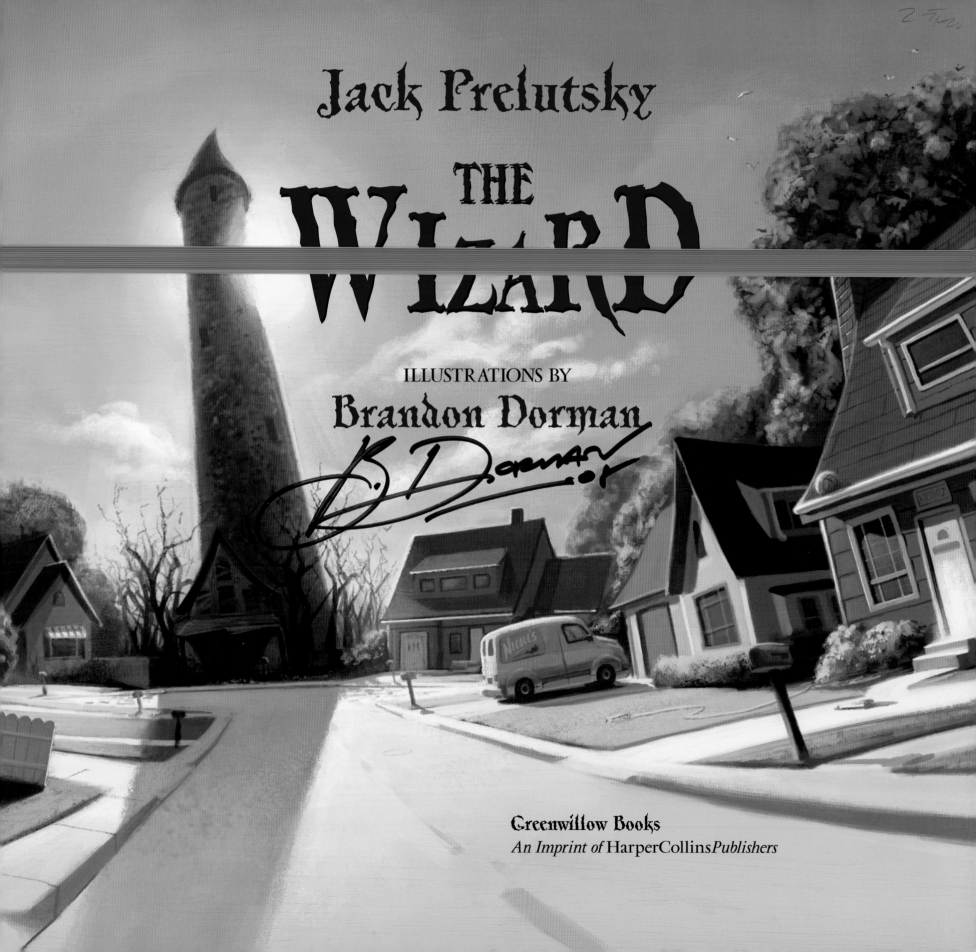

Jack Prelutsky

THE WIZARD

ILLUSTRATIONS BY

Brandon Dorman

Greenwillow Books
An Imprint of HarperCollinsPublishers

The Wizard
Text copyright © 1976, 2007 by Jack Prelutsky
Illustrations copyright © 2007 by Brandon Dorman
All rights reserved. Manufactured in China.
www.harpercollinschildrens.com

Text adapted from "The Wizard," originally published in
Nightmares: Poems to Trouble Your Sleep, Greenwillow Books, 1976.
Digital art was used for the full-color illustrations.
The text type is 21-point Vendome ICG.

Library of Congress Cataloging-in-Publication Data
Prelutsky, Jack.
The wizard / by Jack Prelutsky ; illustrated by Brandon Dorman.
   p. cm.
"Greenwillow Books."
Summary: An illustrated, rhyming tale of a wicked wizard and his
evil deeds, as he uses "elemental sorcery" to change a bullfrog into a
series of objects, from a flea to a flame.
ISBN-13: 978-0-06-124076-8 (trade bdg.) ISBN-10: 0-06-124076-1 (trade bdg.)
ISBN-13: 978-0-06-124077-5 (lib. bdg.) ISBN-10: 0-06-124077-X (lib. bdg.)
[1. Wizards—Fiction. 2. Magic—Fiction. 3. Stories in rhyme.]
I. Dorman, Brandon, ill. II. Title.
PZ8.3.P9Wiz 2007 [E]—dc22 2006022296

First Edition 10 9 8 7 6 5 4 3

▨ Greenwillow Books

In memory of Ted Rand—
a wizard if ever there was
—J. P.

Dedicated to my wonderful
mother and father
—B. D.

The wizard, watchful, waits alone
within his tower of cold gray stone

and ponders in his wicked way
what evil deeds he'll do this day.

He's tall and thin, with wrinkled skin,
a tangled beard hangs from his chin,

his cheeks are gaunt, his eyes set deep,
he scarcely eats, he needs no sleep.

He spies a bullfrog by the door
and, stooping, scoops it off the floor.

He flicks his wand, the frog's a flea
through elemental sorcery.

The flea hops once,
the flea hops twice

the flea becomes a pair of mice
that dive into a bubbling brew,

emerging as one cockatoo.

The wizard laughs a hollow laugh,
the soaking bird's reduced by half,

and when, perplexed, it starts to squawk,
the wizard turns it into chalk

dle Peedle Queedle Quoo!

with which he deftly writes a spell

that makes the chalk a silver bell,

which tinkles in the ashen air
till flash . . . a fire burns brightly there.

He gestures with an ancient knack
to try to bring the bullfrog back.

Another flash! . . . no flame now burns
as once again the frog returns,

but when it bounds about in fear,
the wizard shouts, "Begone from here,"

and midway through a frightened croak
it vanishes in clouds of smoke.

The wizard smirks a fiendish smirk,
reflecting on the woes he'll work,

as he consults a dusty text
and checks which hex he'll conjure next.

He may pluck someone off the spot
and turn him into . . . who knows what?

Should you encounter a toad or lizard,
look closely . . .

it may be the work of the wizard.